ROBINSON CRUSOE
by
DANIEL DEFOE

pictures by N.C.WYETH

ROBINSON CRUSOE

DANIEL DEFOE
illustrated by N. C. WYETH

A SCRIBNER STORYBOOK CLASSIC
Atheneum Books for Young Readers
New York London Toronto Sydney Singapore

Atheneum Books for Young Readers

An imprint of Simon & Schuster Children's Publishing Division

1230 Avenue of the Americas, New York, New York 10020

Abridgement copyright © 2003 by Timothy Meis

Illustrations by N. C. Wyeth. First published 1920.

Book design by Abelardo Martínez

The text for this book is set in Palatino.

The illustrations for this book are rendered in oil.

Manufactured in China

First Edition

2 4 6 8 10 9 7 5 3 1

Library of Congress Cataloging-in-Publication Data

Defoe, Daniel, 1661?–1731.

Robinson Crusoe / Daniel Defoe ; illustrated by N. C. Wyeth.—1st ed.

p.   cm.—(A Scribner storybook classic)

Summary: A diary of an Englishman shipwrecked for almost thirty years on a small isolated
island where, using wit and industry, he manages to build a new life.

ISBN 0-689-85104-9

[1. Shipwrecks—Fiction. 2. Survival—Fiction.] I. Wyeth, N. C. (Newell Convers), 1882–1945, ill.

II. Title. III. Series.

PZ7 .D36 Ro 2003

[Fic]—dc21   2002001937

SEPTEMBER 30, 1659—I POOR, MISERABLE ROBINSON CRUSOE, BEING SHIPWRECKED, DURING A DREADFUL STORM, CAME ON SHORE ON THIS DISMAL, UNFORTUNATE ISLAND WHICH I CALLED THE ISLAND OF DESPAIR.

CHAPTER ONE

I was born in the year 1632 in the city of York, England. My father was originally from Bremen, Germany. He traveled from that land to settle in England, and marry my mother. I was called Robinson Kreutznauer upon my birth. But the people of the English countryside found it easier to pronounce our name differently, and soon we were called the Crusoes.

Very early in life I dreamed of leaving my small town and seeing what the world had to offer me. I longed to ramble, and soon fixed my imagination upon sailing the seas in search of my fortune. My father, however, was against this notion of mine. He believed that I should enter the law profession and stay near to where I was born.

One morning, my father, who was a wise and serious man, called me into his chamber, where he was confined to his bed due to sickness.

"Your mother tells me you wish to leave our house and become a sailor," he began. "I cannot warn you sternly enough what misfortune will befall you if you do what you plan."

"But Father," I interrupted, "you left *your* country as a young man . . ."

"I was poor," he stopped me. "It is for men of little money to go abroad upon adventures." He breathed deeply and closed his eyes. "I have already lost your older brothers to the world; one a soldier who died in a foreign land. The other I have not heard from since he, like you, went to search for his fortune. Would you break your father's heart a third time, Robinson?"

I became choked up and could not answer him, for I loved him so and did not wish to hurt him further.

"If you stay here in York, I will do kind things for you to see that you begin a life of worthwhile work with friends and family around you," he continued. "Do not play the wild young man. I will always pray for you wherever you are, but I cannot promise you that God will protect you if you leave the blessings of your home."

I looked at his face and saw tears running down his cheeks upon the bed cloth. I was so moved by this that I embraced him, and our tears mingled as I promised him that I would never run away and hurt him.

I was so affected by my father's wishes that I resolved to settle at home and give up my dreams of roving. But alas! A few days later it all wore off. I found myself as unhappy as I was before I talked to my father, and decided again that I must go see the world.

My father shook his head and warned me again, "If you go abroad, you will be the most miserable human that was ever born. You leave without my blessing."

But I was of the age that believed the world would open its arms to me and provide me with all the fortune I could ever wish for. When a friend of mine told me he was going to board his father's ship bound for London, I eagerly agreed to join him.

And so early one morning, without asking God's blessing, I exited the door of my home and began a life more miserable than even my father could have ever imagined.

I became choked up and could not answer him. . . .

CHAPTER TWO

On the first of September, 1651, we left for London. The ship was no sooner out of port when the wind began to blow violently. The waves rose to a dreadful height, and the ship was rocked to and fro in the storm. As I had never been to sea before, I was very sick, and terrified as to what would become of the ship and me. I expected that every wave would swallow us up. At that moment I vowed that if I again reached dry land, I would rush home to my father, beg his forgiveness, and promise to wander no more.

Throughout the night the storm continued, as did my unbearable seasickness. But by the next day, the wind stilled and I was able to sleep. Soon I was as cheerful as I ever was on solid land. I looked with wonder upon the sea. Just last night it was so terrible and rough, and now it was as calm as a small lake.

The surface of the sea was so smooth and gentle that I presently forgot my vow to return to my father. I felt as though my fortunes had improved, and that I had again found favor with the world. The idea of being swallowed up by a wave had left my mind, as did any thought to return home.

It was on the sixth day of our being at sea that a terrible storm arose, more violent than the first. Our sails slapped ferociously, our rope lines lashed helplessly in the dark, and the boat itself creaked as though at any instant the storm would crack our vessel in half. I saw terror and amazement in the faces of the sailors. The waves rose like mountains and broke upon us every few minutes.

We had a sturdy ship, but the sailors about me shouted that she would not last long.

"She'll founder!" they yelled as they attempted to secure lines and sails. "Sure as your life, she'll founder!" I suppose it was to my advantage that I had so little knowledge of the sea that I did not know what they meant by "founder."

Soon it became apparent that the ship would never make it back to port. The captain began to fire the large guns in hopes that a passing ship might hear us and come to our aid. Eventually a light ship heard our distress and sent out a small boat to help us. Our men cast out a rope over the stern to them. The men in the small boat grabbed hold of it and we hauled them closer to our ship.

In between the rising of each wave, we abandoned our ship and lowered ourselves down into the smaller vessel. We made our way slowly to shore, disembarked, and walked all the way to the English town of Yarmouth.

We were not much more than a quarter of an hour out of our ship when we saw her sink. It was then that I understood for the first time what was meant by a ship foundering at sea.

Had I now had the sense to return to York and the bosom of my family, I no doubt would have had a happy life. But it was as though a cloud of black fate had hung over me since I left my home. And, as I found out, it was to remain over me for many years that would follow. It was as though I had a secret urging within me, enticing me toward my own destruction.

I confessed these thoughts to my friend not long after we found shelter in his father's house. His father felt that it was his duty to warn me, "Young man, if you do not go back to your home, wherever you go you will meet nothing but disasters, till your father's words are fulfilled."

I have since observed how irrational youth can be. Why was I not ashamed to leave, but ashamed to return to my father and admit my mistakes? But I think that many are their own worst enemies. Such was the case where I was concerned. Heeding neither my friend's father's advice, nor that of my own father, I boarded a vessel bound for the coast of Africa. It was on this trip that

I learned a love and respect for the sea. I was instructed by the captain of the vessel on how to keep an account of the ship's course, take an observation, and learn all the things necessary for a sailor to stay alive at sea.

I returned from this trip a slightly richer man than when I left, so I resolved to double my fortune and take the same voyage again. I embarked on the same vessel with most of the same crew, and yet, this was one of the unhappiest travels I set out upon in my short life. As our ship made its way toward the Canary Islands, we were surprised by a Turkish pirate ship. Up to that point I had only heard tales of Barbary pirates, but from the tales the other sailors told, I knew they were fierce fighters. As we prepared for battle, the pirates approached us quickly from the bow with their muskets drawn.

I had the task of bringing the gunpowder to the men on deck and so made my way from man to man with the small keg of powder, ever mindful of the advancing pirate ship. Once the pirates drew in closer, we poured a full broadside in upon them with all our twelve guns. But they were determined to steal our ship and cargo, and, braving the cannon fire, came up alongside our vessel and boarded it. Sixty of those barbarous men slashed and hacked their way onboard, cutting the decks and rigging. We shot at them with our muskets, fowling pieces, and anything that fired a ball. The ship was soon covered in a haze of gun smoke and the air was full of shots, groans, and the screams of men cut with a sword or hit by a musket ball. We fought gallantly, but they soon disabled our ship. Three of our men were killed and eight were wounded. We were forced to give up the ship and all that was on board. The Turkish pirates carried us into slavery into the Sallee, a port belonging to the Moors.

CHAPTER THREE

I was made a slave to a powerful Turk at the emperor's court. Though I had never before seen such wealth, I was extremely unhappy at being forced to do what I did not want. My youthful desire to be free and go where I pleased had not left me and soon I began to think about how I would escape.

Two years had passed before I was able to put into action my plan to flee the Moorish country. My master, who loved to fish, always took me and a young boy with him to row his boat when he went out upon the ocean. Since I knew my way around the sea, and was adept at fishing, my master prized my company.

One day the Moor ordered me and the boy, whose name was Xury, to prepare the boat. I put into the boat a large basket of biscuits and three jars of fresh water. This was not out of the ordinary, for the Moor enjoyed eating during the many hours we usually spent at sea.

After we had fished for some time, I said to the Moor, "We must fish farther from the shore. That is where the large fish gather."

He agreed with my suggestion and stood to help me with the sail. I felt as though my chance had at last come, and so I seized it!

I grabbed him by his waist and, with a quick toss, threw him overboard. He bounced up like a cork and begged to be taken back on board. I reached for an oar and held it menacingly over my head.

"You swim well enough to reach the shore," I shouted. "And the sea is calm. Start swimming and do not turn back toward the boat. I am an Englishman, and I will have my liberty!" So, he uttered what I believed to be some sort of Moorish curse, turned himself around, and swam for shore.

After he swam fifty yards from the boat I turned to Xury, who was staring wide-eyed at me. But before I could open my mouth, he begged to go along with me and not be thrown overboard. He swore his faithfulness to me again and again, and promised that he would go all over the world with me if I did not send him back to shore. His eyes were so innocent and his voice so earnest, that I could not have distrusted him if I wanted to.

I hoisted the sail and caught a fair wind for the rest of that day. By the next morning, we were far from the reach of my previous master and the land of the Moors.

Xury and I sailed for over a week in our small vessel. We kept close to the coast since we had no instruments to sail by, and were always on the lookout for pirates or ships that might try to return us to slavery. My plan was to sail as far as the Cape de Verde, where I hoped to meet up with some European ship. I was determined, and said so to Xury, that we must find a ship or die trying.

After a number of days with our sail full to the wind, I decided to sleep a spell. Not long after I was awoken by the lad crying out, "Master, master! A ship with a sail!"

I jumped out of the cabin and instantly recognized the shape of the bow and the cut of the sail. It was a Portuguese ship. With all the sail I could make, I headed toward the vessel and reached it in three hours' time.

Both Xury and I boarded the vessel and were welcomed with great cheer by the sailors. It was an inexpressible joy to me to meet such kindly faces that would deliver me from slavery and certain death upon the sea. They then inquired as to what language I spoke. "Portuguese?" they asked.

"No," I said.

"Spanish?"

"No."

"French?"

Again I said no.

At last a Scottish sailor called out to me and I joyfully answered him.

"I am an Englishman," I said. "My ship was captured by pirates and I was sold into slavery by the Moors at Sallee."

I offered the captain my boat in a form of payment for passage on their ship.

"No, no, Seignior Inglese," he said, addressing me as "Mister English." "We are on our way to Brazil in the Americas. When we get there, you can sell your boat so that you can pay for your journey back to England."

I thanked him kindly for his generosity.

"Seignior Inglese," he continued, "I will pay you sixty pieces of eight, which is the money of my country, for the boy you have there."

I was very sad to sell poor Xury's liberty, but I felt as though I could trust this captain to be fair to him. I also knew I would need the money to return to York.

"I will sell you the boy," I said, "if you promise that you will release him in ten years' time if he becomes a Christian."

The captain readily agreed, and Xury had no quarrel with this arrangement. He had been born a slave and had never known freedom in his life. Were I to set him free, he would not know how to get on in the world, and would most likely return to the Moors because they were the only people he knew. I was confident that this captain would teach him much about the sea, and after ten years' time, he would know more about sailing than I did, and would be able to make a life for himself.

Our voyage to Brazil took twenty-two days. I bid my shipmates and my friend Xury good-bye, sold my boat, and purchased an ingeino to live in. After talking with some farmers, who told me how easy it would be to make my fortune on the land, I quickly gave up all thoughts of returning to England until I had done so. I bought a small sugar cane plantation, and worked hard on it for several years. Eventually it became a large plantation. I increased my wealth but found that in one important way I was no richer, living all alone in the center of an enormous stretch of land. Like a man cast away on a desolate island, I longed to converse with someone.

I began to venture into the seaport of St. Salvador to meet with other planters, as well as sea merchants. I had learned a bit of both Spanish and Portuguese, so I could speak to them of many things, including my travels. I told them of my two voyages to the coast of Guinea where I had traded with the Negroes there. My friends were swept away by my tales of inexpensive purchases of gold dust, grains, and elephants' teeth.

Swearing me to secrecy, my fellow planters told me that they wanted to fit a ship and sail to Guinea. Since I knew the ways of this foreign land, they begged me to sign on board. I know I should have said no and remained in Brazil where I was wealthy and prosperous, but alas I did not. Being born to be my own destroyer, I found I was as helpless to refuse my friends as I had been to stop my earlier ramblings. Again I should have listened to my father's words of advice, but I did not. I told them I would go.

CHAPTER FOUR

I went on board the first of September, 1659, it being the same day eight years earlier that I had left my mother and father in York. Almost immediately a violent storm broke upon us, carrying us westward. Our crew of eleven men, including myself, was helpless to redirect our course, and we worried about landing on an island full of savages.

With this in our thoughts, one morning one of the men cried out, "Land!" We no sooner had run out of the cabin to look, when our ship struck something, flinging us forward. Then it stopped entirely. We had hit a sand bar and could go neither forward nor backward, although the fierce wind continued to push us as though it had designs to capsize the ship and scuttle the lives of all the men on board.

As the ship leaned dangerously to one side, we slung a small boat we had on board over the side of our vessel. We slid down ropes into the boat and tried to row the tiny craft, but in the storm we were tossed about like a child's plaything. When we were about a league and a half from our stranded ship, a raging, mountainlike wave came rolling over us. It flipped the boat and tossed all eleven of us into the depths. We were separated and cast under the frothing tide.

Nothing can describe the panic I felt when I hit the water. I gasped for air, but succeeded in only drawing saltwater down my throat. A wave drove me like a giant hand and swept me onto a piece of hard land, a rock! The pain when I hit was enormous, but I grabbed hold of the rock and drew myself onto it. I looked up and saw an island before me. I attempted to stand, but when I started to straighten up, I vomited all the water that filled my lungs and sunk back down. I had just struggled to my feet again when another wave took me in itself and dashed me upon the ocean floor. I found it was impossible to swim out of it, so I held my breath and waited for it to release me.

Finally, I bobbed up like a cork and filled my lungs with precious air when another wave smashed over me, burying me twenty or thirty feet deep in its own body, carrying me swiftly toward the shore.

I was ready to burst with holding my breath, when I again shot out above the surface of the water. I lunged forward before the return of the next wave and felt the sandy ground with my feet. Again I was dashed against a piece of rock, but knowing that my salvation was close at hand, I held on to that rock and pulled myself onto the mainland.

Utterly exhausted, and with every muscle seemingly bruised, I stumbled up the cliffs on the shore and sat down on a piece of grass, finally free from the grip of the water.

After resting but a moment, I raced up and down the shore with the wind lashing my face, looking for my comrades. But there was not a one to be found. Eleven men had entered that small boat, but I alone survived to make it to land. I cast my eyes on the stranded ship that lay stuck in the sand bar, still heaving under the power of the wind and waves. It seemed so far off, and I thought to myself, Lord! How was it possible that I made it to shore safely?

I immediately thought to find some shelter and water to drink so I reluctantly left the beach and set off into an opening in the trees just beyond the shore. Though the vegetation was thick, it did not hurt as much as the whipping wind in the open air. I soon found a small stream of fresh water, and, crouching, drank and drank. Having nothing with me but a knife, a tobacco pipe and a little tobacco in a box in my coat pocket, I placed the tobacco into my mouth to keep my hunger at bay. As darkness fell, I found a low-lying tree nearby the stream and climbed into it. I wedged myself between two stout limbs that would keep me from falling, and, assured that I would waken if any strange beasts should try to surprise me, I welcomed sleep.

CHAPTER FIVE

When I awoke, it was broad daylight and the weather had cleared. The storm had blown out to sea. The ship still lay a good mile out beyond the land. I once again scanned the shoreline for any of my companions, but saw none. From where I stood, it was a direct course from the ship to the island. If any of the men had survived the capsizing of our tiny boat, they would either have washed out to sea, or past this little beach where I stood, and hence, entirely past the island itself.

I cursed this misfortune but resolved to swim out to see if by some happy chance, some of the men had made it back to the ship. I pulled off my clothes, and dove into the water. Swimming out to the vessel, I circled her twice, calling out to my comrades. But there was no reply. Sad at heart, I circled again, looking for a way to get on board. I was fast growing tired when I spied a small piece of rope that hung down from the stern of the ship. With great difficulty I got hold of it and pulled myself up into the ship.

I shouted "Halloo!" several times, hoping against hope for a reply. But no man's voice answered back. Going below, I saw that there was a great deal of water in the ship's hold. And yet, most of her provisions were dry and untouched. I proceeded to the breadroom and ate my fill of biscuits, and stuffed my pockets with more.

As I prepared to return to the deck I heard a scraping sound in one of the rooms. It was faint at first, and I could barely hear it over the creaking of the stranded ship and the waves lapping against its side. But as I made my way closer to the captain's cabin, the noise became louder. I even thought I heard the sound of rapid breathing. I admit that I was rather frightened because it did not sound like a man.

"Halloo!" I said softly, too afraid to raise my voice.

There was no answer from behind the door, only more scraping against wood. I envisioned hideous sea monsters had somehow gotten through a hole in the ship's bottom and were now trying to infest the entire ship.

I braced myself with a deep breath to muster up my courage.

"Halloo!" I shouted. A bark and a howl went up from the captain's cabin.

I waited but an instant before I realized what it was scratching behind the door—the captain's dog! I raced to the cabin, threw open the door, and was greeted with a hearty welcome. The canine leapt on me, and licked my hands and face in such an eager manner that I supposed he was saying thank you in his own way. I took some biscuits out of my pockets and fed him. Before long, two cats had come out of their hiding places beneath a table and rubbed their bodies against my legs. I took some comfort in knowing that there was some sign of life still on this wrecked boat, even though it wasn't human.

Returning above, I threw five large spars of wood overboard, and tied them together with some strong rope. I made them into the shape of a raft the best I could. Laying three more pieces of plank upon them cross-ways, I found I could walk upon it very well.

I next had to decide what to load onto the raft. I first got three of the seaman's wooden chests. The first I filled with bread, rice, three Dutch cheeses, five pieces of dried goat's flesh, and a little European corn. After long searching I found the carpenter's chest full of tools, which I thought would prove useful to me. I took all the men's clothes that I could find, a spare fore-top sail, a hammock, and some bedding. There were also muskets, fowling pieces, shot, and three barrels of gunpowder; two were good, but the third had taken water.

I found a Bible, which I thought might provide me with something to read, and some paper and pens. I carried the cats with me, but the dog jumped overboard and swam to shore alongside my raft. What little wind there was, helped blow me to shore. I spied a small creek that I hoped to use as a port to land safely without upsetting my load, and set my raft toward it, and with the help of the current, I entered the creek. At length I noticed a small cove on the right shore of the creek. I guided my raft with the oar until I could thrust the small vessel into the cove and onto dry land.

The next work I set myself to do was to search the countryside for a proper place to make a home. I still had no idea where I was, or whether the land was inhabited with savages and wild beasts. There was a hill, not a mile northward from me that I thought would be a good place to get a look at the island. I set out with one of the pistols, a horn of powder, and some shot. The going was rough in that I needed to make a trail through the vast shrubs, vine growth, and trees that covered the island.

At long last I reached the top of the hill and confirmed my suspicions that I was indeed on an island covered on all sides by the sea. Worse yet, there were no islands nearby, and none on the horizon. A wave of loneliness and despair rushed over me and grasped my heart with such a power I had never before felt. Compared to this, the agony I felt on the shore when I realized none of my companions were saved was but a mere passing discomfort.

I resolved to return to my raft and begin my occupation of this Island of Despair, as I named it. On the walk back, I shot at a great bird which I saw sitting in a tree. I believe it was the first gun that had been fired there since the creation of the world. As for the creature I killed, I took it to be a kind of a hawk.

I made it back to the raft and began to unload my cargo onto the shore. After barricading myself around with the chests and the boards, and making a kind of a hut for that night's lodging, I fell asleep. But my heart was heavy and I had a restless slumber.

CHAPTER SIX

*E*ach morning at low tide I returned to the ship that lay off shore and tried to bring away everything I could possibly transport: small ropes and rope twine, a piece of spare canvas, the barrel of wet gunpowder, and all the sails. I had now been on shore thirteen days, and eleven times back on board the ship. Had the weather remained calm, I think I could have brought ashore the entire vessel piece by piece. But as I was preparing the twelfth time to sail out, I found the sky overcast and the wind beginning to rise. I abandoned my plan, and as I lay in the tent I had made out of the sail, the wind blew hard all that night. In the morning when I looked out, the ship was nearly fully sunk.

Knowing that weather could be harsh in this part of the world with hurricanes and excessive heat, I set about finding a better spot of ground for a more permanent shelter. I considered what I needed most. First, fresh water, second, shelter from the heat of the sun, third, security from deadly creatures and finally, a view of the sea. I found a little plain on the side of a rising hill that was ideal. Nearby was a hollow place in the hill, like the entrance to a cave.

On the flat of the green, I drew a half circle around the hollow place. In this half circle I drove two rows of strong stakes into the ground till they stood very firm like spears, sharpened on top. They formed the "wall" of my new habitation. The entrance into this place I made with a ladder, not a door. In this way I could lift the ladder in after me, and keep everything else out.

Into this little fortress I carried all my provisions, ammunitions, and sails. I made a large tent of canvas and set up the hammock that was used previously by a mate on the ship. When this work was done, I dug out the hollow area so that it more resembled a small cave or cellar where I could store things.

I went out daily with my gun, partly to find something to eat, but also so

I spied a small creek. . . .

that I could better acquaint myself with the island. I was pleased to discover that there were goats on the island. But when I tried to shoot them for meat, they were so shy and so swift of foot, that I could not get near enough to fire on them. After chasing them a number of times in vain, I learned that if I shot at the goats from the rocks above them, they never saw me. But if I approached them from the valley, they would see me and flee. I supposed it must have something to do with them always looking down while they are grazing.

My first successful shot hit a she-goat with its kid nearby. The bleating young goat stood by until I came to pick up the mother, and it followed me back to my enclosure. I took the kid in hopes that I could breed it and that it would be tame. Alas, it would not eat, and so I was forced to slaughter it and eat it myself. These two goats supplied me with meat for a great while.

Slowly, I was becoming used to my island. Yet I still found time to be depressed over my lot in life. Tears would run down my cheeks when I thought that Providence, that is, God's will, would utterly abandon me with no human company at all. But whenever I withdrew too deeply into these sad thoughts, a voice inside me would ask, "Though you are poorly off, where are the rest of your shipmates? Why were you saved and not them?" This would cheer me up to a degree, but never to the point where I was happy.

After I had been here several weeks, it occurred to me that I might lose all track of time if I did not mark the days. I set up a large post on the rocks so that it was secure, and fixed a plank across its top in the shape of a cross. With my knife I carved the words "I came on shore here on the 30th of September, 1659," onto the wood. On the sides of the square post I cut a notch for every day I was there. Every seventh notch was made slightly larger so that I could keep track of weeks, months, and eventually years. It gave me some satisfaction to make this calendar, and even though the years might pass in the world outside my island, I would know that they did not escape without my noticing them.

With my knife I carved the words, "I came on shore here on the 30th of September, 1659."

CHAPTER SEVEN

*A*s my time continued on the island, I began to construct things that I would use every day, wanting to reconstruct as much of the world that I left behind as I could. I realized very quickly that I would need a table and chair. It would have to be entirely of my own creation, and I was to start from scratch.

So I went to work. I had never handled a tool in my life, but I became more and more adept as I cut down tree limbs and sawed and hammered. And after many nicks and cuts on my hands, I had a table and chair in the hollow of my little castle.

My work days, though full of hard labor, were relatively short because I had no candles to light my work at night. I was forced to go to sleep each night when the sun fell. But after I had killed several goats, I realized I could save the tallow, that is the fat, and store it in a little dish of clay that I had baked in the sun. To the tallow I added a wick of some oakum and made myself a lamp.

One day while I was cleaning all my supplies to make sure no vermin were infesting my castle, I found a little bag. I thought that I should be able to use it while out adventuring around the island and so emptied the few husks out of it onto the ground. Soon afterward I saw a few stalks of something green shooting out from the ground. And a few weeks afterward, to my delight, I saw ten or twelve ears of green barley sprout out.

There is no way to accurately describe my astonishment at seeing this growth. Before this moment I had few thoughts of religion. But after I saw the barley grow there, in a climate not proper for corn, I began to notice the hand of God in this work. Could he have caused this grain to grow so that I might eat in this wild, miserable place? This thought brought tears of joy to my eyes, and I thanked Providence. When the barley ripened, I saved all the ears, and ate none of them, so that they could all be replanted. In time I hoped they might provide me with enough grain to supply me with bread. It was not until the fourth year that I allowed myself to eat some of the grain.

One afternoon as I was busy cleaning out and expanding my cave, I heard a terrible rumbling above and around me. Earth began to fall from the roof of my cave and from the edge of the hill over my head. My heart leapt and I struggled to regain my breath as I tried to understand what was happening.

I ran out of the cave, up the ladder, and over the fence. I no sooner stepped off the ladder when the ground shook three times. It was an earthquake, something I had heard sailors speak of! The motion of the earth made my stomach sick, as though I were being tossed at sea again. Rock began to shear off the side of my hill and plunge into the sea. I wasn't sure whether to fling myself to the ground or run.

After the third shock was over I began to take some courage. But I was scared to go back into my enclosure for fear of being buried alive. I sat upon the ground, greatly downcast and depressed, unsure of what to do.

As I sat and stared at my little home that had proven so untrustworthy in the face of an earthquake I said aloud, "Lord! What a miserable creature am I!" Then the tears burst forth from my eyes and I could say little for a good while.

At length the advice of my father came to my mind; that is if I took the foolish step to leave our happy home, God would not bless me. "Now," I whispered between my tears, "my dear father's words are come to pass." Then I shouted, "Lord, be my help, for I am in great distress." That was my first prayer, if I can call it that, since I was a young boy.

So it was that day that I took up the Bible, and began to read. The first words I came across were these: "Call on Me in the day of trouble, and I will deliver thee, and thou shalt glorify Me." These words made a great impression on me.

I read until it grew late. But before I lay down, I did what I had never done in all my life. I kneeled down and prayed to God to fulfill his promise to me; that if I called upon Him in my day of trouble, that He would deliver me.

CHAPTER EIGHT

When I awoke the next day, I found my spirit refreshed and my heart lighter than it had been the day before. I arose and felt stronger as well. My thoughts ran again to the passage from scripture, "I will deliver thee." And so I asked myself the question: "Had I not been delivered from the quake?" The answer was obviously "Yes!" But I felt as though I had not yet done my part. He delivered me, but I did not glorify Him. No, I had not thanked him.

It touched my heart immensely to know that God watched over me and kept me safe, and I immediately kneeled and thanked him with all the kind words I knew.

And so began my reading of the Bible. Each morning I awoke, and, beginning with the New Testament, began to seriously read it. Also, at night I would read it until my thoughts wandered and I fell into sleep.

I had now been on this unhappy island over ten months and all chance of leaving it seemed impossible. I firmly believed that no human had ever set foot on this ground before me, and none would ever again. And yet, my own family grew. I was upset with the disappearance of one of my cats, who I thought ran away from me and was now dead. But one day at about the end of August she returned with three kittens. I scooped them all up in pleasure and held them close.

This new life gave me the excitement and will to explore more of my island. I took my gun, a hatchet, my dog, a larger quantity of shot than usual, and began my journey. I spent several days adventuring and even made it to the other side of the island where I had a view of the sea to the west.

While out exploring I saw a number of parrots. I stalked them for hours, and finally captured a small one with a net I had woven from canvas thread.

I sat upon the ground, greatly downcast and depressed. . . .

The seashore on the opposite side of the island was covered with hundreds of turtles. There were also so many different kinds of fowl that I was not able to count all the types. I could have shot as many as I pleased, but I didn't want to waste any of my powder—it was better to use the gunpowder to down a goat, which would provide more meat.

While I found that this side of the island was much more pleasant, I had no desire to move here. Where I was had become home to me, no matter how crude it was. And so I ventured back to my home with the parrot. I was happy to return.

And so my life continued on, developing into a fairly routine schedule of Bible reading, searching for and preparing food, protecting myself and my home from the weather, and attempting to teach the parrot to speak. Still, it was years before it could say its own name, "Poll," Day after day the tides rolled in with no hope of rescue in sight. While I had grown accustomed to my island, I still longed to interact with someone or something outside my little world.

The rainy season of the autumnal equinox came with the anniversary of my landing on the Island of Despair, the thirtieth of September. I had been here two whole years. Although my heart was sad with loneliness, I spent the day giving thanks to God.

And so began my reading of the Bible.

CHAPTER NINE

*M*ost of my days on the island were employed with trying to make my life more pleasant. The corn grew more plentiful than I could have imagined. When I saw the amount of grain that I could harvest, I realized I needed containers to store it in, as well as earthen vessels to prepare my meals.

I found what looked to me to be suitable clay near the inlet where I first sailed ashore. It was tawny in color and lumpy in texture. I dug it, tempered it, brought it home, worked it with my hands until my knuckles throbbed, and then baked it in the sun. And yet, what with all the work I invested in this enterprise, I succeeded in making only two large unsightly vessels. But oh, what joy these ugly pots brought me. And when I found that I could boil water and some meat in them, my delight doubled.

Though I kept my hands busy with projects such as the clay pots, my mind began to focus on escaping the island. I decided that if I could build a chair and table, then surely I could build a canoe and sail away from here.

I thought back to my days in Brazil and remembered seeing a number of native canoes made from the trunk of a single tree. So I set out to find a proper tree, large enough to seat me, my dog, and whatever food stuffs I should bring along, comfortably. At last I came upon a tall cedar, suitable for my plans. It was five feet, ten inches wide at the lower part, next to the stump, and four feet eleven inches wide at the end of twenty-two feet. It took me twenty days to fell it with my hatchet, and fourteen more to clear it of branches and limbs. Three months were spent clearing out the inside. This I did without the use of fire, though I have seen the natives do so. Instead, I used a mallet and chisel from my tool chest.

When I had finished my work, I stood back and felt very pleased with what I had accomplished.

The corn grew more plentifully than I could have imagined.

It was during the construction of this canoe that I marked the fourth anniversary of my imprisonment on this island.

Through these years my clothes began to decay. Though the weather was always warm, I could not go around naked due to the ever-present sun that blistered my skin. So, I wove together a rough suit of goat skin and even a cap, because the sun on my bare head gave me terrible headaches. I even made myself an umbrella. I had seen them used in Brazil to allow one to always carry the shade with them. It proved very useful in the great heat.

As I completed my boat, my next thought was to make a tour around the island, such as a king might ride around his kingdom. I was very eager to see the opposite side of the island from the water, and to see how my canoe would fare on the open sea. I fitted a mast to it and made a small sail out of the sail of the ship that had brought me to this island. After rigging the sail to the mast, I fixed my umbrella at the stern to keep the heat of the sun off me.

It was on the sixth of November, in the sixth year of my reign, or captivity, that I pushed my vessel into the water. The canoe handled nicely until I sailed a league out from the shore and found myself in deeper water. This deep water whisked me away from the island so quickly I feared I would lose sight of it entirely.

I was caught in an ebb tide. As it pulled me farther and farther away from my home, I worked frantically with all my might. I pulled the sail tight until my muscles groaned. Again and again I repositioned my sail to catch the wind to draw the boat and me out of the violent current, yet, to my continual frustration, the canoe was still being drawn out into the open sea.

If the current succeeded in taking me away from the sight of my home, I would never be able to make my way back because I had no compass on board. I was determined not to let this happen; I knew I couldn't bear to be lost again. I took off my rudder and attempted to use it as an oar. I rowed until the

I began to steer my boat toward shore.

muscles in my shoulders screamed out, but still the boat moved away from the island. Soon I could barely lift my arms, but I refused to give up. I lowered my head and tore into the water with my oar, yelling in pain with each stroke.

At last a fresh breeze arose. I quickly replaced my rudder and attempted to capture this gale with my sail. When the sail filled, I pulled the line I had attached to it taut and began to steer my boat toward shore. The wind kept up enough to get me out of the current and allowed me to sail the boat into an inlet which narrowed into a small brook. This was a perfect harbor for my boat.

Having stowed my boat safely among some vines that grew near the water, I got out on the shore to see where I was. I fell to my knees, and in my exhaustion thanked God for my deliverance. Again I thought how easily I could have been lost to life had not the hand of God delivered me at the moment I needed Him most. I never again ventured into that canoe, and gave up the time that I spent working on it as lost.

CHAPTER TEN

*I*n the eleventh year of my residence, I decided to capture a she-goat with young so that I might raise them. I dug several large pits in the earth, and over this I spread a collection of branches and palm fronds. On top of these I placed a few ears of barley and dry rice. When I went out one morning to inspect my traps, I found a she-goat with three kids, a male and two females, within them. Taking the goats one by one, I tied strings around their necks and brought them home.

It was a good while before they would eat, but I eventually tempted them with some sweet corn. They grew tame, and I realized that if I were to have meat after my powder and shot ran out, then I would have to continue breeding these animals. My traps caught me several more goats, including a male, and in about a year and a half, I had a flock of about twelve goats. In two more years, I had forty-three.

I had begun to grow accustomed to life on the island, the weather, cultivating grain, and watching over my flock of goats. It was a simple life, relatively free from worry, and I felt that it was possible for me to live till the end of my days and not see another human. All of this changed one day as I walked along the shore.

Since I had given up the idea of seeing the whole of the island by boat, I resolved to walk along its shore until I had seen it all. The day began similarly to all the others I had previously spent on this island, so I was not prepared for what I saw clearly upon the seashore.

There before me in the sand was the perfect impression of a man's foot. I stood like one thunderstruck. It was not my footprint, for it was too small. And no beast could have made the mark either. No, another human being had set

foot upon my island. A chill passed over me as I looked up and down the shoreline to see if this man was still around and watching me.

I saw no one. Mistaking every bush and tree at a distance to be a man, I hurried home to my fortification. I was terrified. I did not know what to make of this invasion of my island. Was it someone who could save me and take me back to civilization? Or was it a savage who landed here?

After a night without sleep, I concluded that it must be a savage. But I could not answer the question, "Was he still here on the island?" And if not, would he return with more men? I would never feel safe again here if I thought savages might find me.

These thoughts took up many hours and days, and even weeks and months. I was constantly uneasy until I repeated these words from scripture: "Call upon Me in the day of trouble, and I will deliver thee, and thou shalt glorify Me." Upon reading this passage my heart would find comfort and this encouraged me to pray to God for deliverance.

As I began to think more clearly, I concluded that this island was not so abandoned as I had previously thought it to be. And so I set off again walking around it, this time with my perspective glass in hand in case I should spy a ship or a savage. When I came to the south west point of the island, I saw upon the sand many skulls, hands, feet, and other human bones, but no one living.

My stomach grew sick from the horrible sight. I dashed back to my hill and did not find comfort till I was safe again in my home.

I reasoned that I had lived there eighteen years already without seeing another human, and it might be another eighteen years before I saw another one. I began to live just as before, except that I used more caution in whatever I did. I avoided as often as possible driving a nail or sawing a board or even firing a gun in case it made too much noise and awoke a savage somewhere on

There before me in the sand was the perfect impression of a man's foot.

my island. I also was uneasy with making any fire, lest the smoke should alert some canoe to my presence. No longer would I do as I pleased on my island. Now everything I did was carefully considered.

Later, my watchfulness paid off, for I was prepared when my island *was* invaded by savages—more than I ever imagined.

I was now in my twenty-third year of residence on this island and could have been content to spend the rest of my life there. I had some amusements, which made the time pass more pleasantly. I taught Poll, my parrot, to speak, and he lived with me twenty-six years. My dog was also a loving companion to me for roughly sixteen years until he died of old age.

As for the cats, they all ran wild into the woods except for two or three favorites of mine. These I kept tame and were part of my family. Plus, I also had two or three kids around me that I taught to feed out of my hand. My life grew again calm.

So one night when the weather was exceptionally foul, I was particularly surprised by the sound of a gun fired at sea. I set down the Bible I was reading and rushed outside to scan the horizon. I saw nothing in the darkness, but I was sure that the gunfire came from a ship in distress.

I quickly gathered all the dry wood I could lay hold of and set it on fire. I was certain that if it were a ship in trouble, then they would see my fire. And as soon as my flames blazed up, I heard another gun, and after that several others, all from the same distant point on the horizon. I fed my fire all night until dawn broke, when at last I saw something out a great distance at sea.

To my great sorrow, it was the wreck of a ship. I ran to the shore to look for survivors, but found none. I imagined that last night they must have seen my light and tried to make for the island in small boats. But with the water being rough they must have capsized and perished.

I cannot explain the longing I felt in my soul and I cried aloud, "Oh, had there been just one soul saved! Just one person that I could have spoken with, just one!" In all the time on this island by myself, I had never wanted company more than I did at that instant. I carried this mournful thought with me for quite some time. Indeed, it became like a silent companion to me.

Then, one morning as I was hunting in the woods near the shore, I spied with the help of my perspective glass no less than five canoes, filled with natives, coming to shore on my side of the island. The savages came four, six, and sometimes more in a boat. I knew I could not attack thirty men single-handedly, so I lay still.

They kindled a fire on the shore and were moving around it in a strange, grotesque way. After the flames had reached a certain height, they dragged two miserable wretches from the boats. One of them was knocked to the ground with a club. Upon seeing this, the other leapt from his captors and sprinted across the sand.

I was horrified to see that he was heading right toward me, followed by two pursuers. But I stayed my ground, hidden in the foliage. At that moment I felt as though I was being called by God to save that poor creature's life. I gathered my two guns, and at the moment he dashed past me, I sprang from my cover and surprised his attackers.

I knocked the first down with the butt of my gun. His companion stopped and stared at me. I did not want to fire my gun because I might alert the others on the shore, but when I saw him fitting an arrow to his bow, I had no choice. I leveled my rifle and killed him with my first shot.

The poor captive, who I saved, stopped in his tracks. Though he saw both his enemies fallen and killed, he neither came forward nor backward. I made signs for him to come closer, which he seemed to understand. He came a little way, then stopped, and then came a little farther, then stopped again. Slowly

he came nearer and nearer, kneeling down every ten or twelve steps, in some sort of thanks for saving his life.

At last he was close to me, and taking my foot, placed it upon his head. I assumed that this was some way of showing me that he was now my slave. Assured that he now trusted me, I hurried him away from that part of the island in case the others who came on shore should try to find him.

At my cave I gave him goat meat and bread to eat, and water to drink. I made signs for him to lie down and sleep, which he did after a short while.

As he slept, I made my way to the top of the hill with my spyglass. I looked all about for the canoes and savages on the shore but saw none. I concluded that they must have left soon after they found their dead friends.

I spied with the help of my perspective glass no less than five canoes. . . .

CHAPTER ELEVEN

*M*y new companion was a handsome fellow with straight, strong limbs, and long black hair. His skin was also very dark. His face was round and plump, with thin lips and fine ivory-colored teeth, his nose small. After he had slept a number of hours, he awoke and made motions, such as lowering his head before me, that I understood to mean that he'd serve me for as long as he lived. Yet I was so overjoyed to have a companion after these long years that I couldn't do enough for him.

I immediately began to teach him how to speak English. First I taught him to say the name I had given him—Friday, for it was on Friday that I rescued him. He seemed happy with the name and quickly learned to say simple words such as "yes" and "no."

I gave him a pair of linen drawers, then made him a cap out of hare skin, and a jerkin from the hide of a goat. At first he found this sleeveless jacket difficult to wear because he was used to going about near naked. But at length he came to enjoy the garment, and was even a bit proud of it.

I realized that it was necessary to increase the amount of grain I grew since there were now two mouths to feed. I marked out a larger plot of land and began to plant more seed. Friday worked very hard at the harvest when the corn became ripe, but he never let on that the work caused him strain or hardship. Instead, he always had a smile upon his face to show me how happy he was to share my labor. And so we gathered the barley, and together enjoyed a great amount of bread.

He even helped me when I went out hunting. I taught him how to fire a gun and was surprised at what a level aim he had. Soon he was almost as good a shot as I was. In truth he was a better hunter because he could get closer to the

At last he was close to me, and taking my foot, placed it upon his head.

prey. More than once I was amazed at how stealthily he could walk, nearly silently, through the woods. He could get so close that he rarely missed when we hunted fowl.

And so began the most pleasant year of life that I had on my island. Friday's simple honesty appeared to me more and more every day. And as he came to understand more English, he began to ask me questions.

"From where you come?" he asked in his broken English.

"Originally from Great Britain," I told him, though I knew he could not comprehend a land so far away. "Recently from Brazil."

"How you come?"

"I sailed in a large boat full of other men like myself."

Friday shook his head as though he understood, but I was not sure he did.

"Would you like to see what is left of our ship?" I asked.

He grinned in reply, and so I led him down to the shoreline. I took out my spyglass and showed him the ruins of our boat, which had now fallen to pieces. Upon seeing this, Friday said, "Me see such a boat like that come to my nation."

I grasped his arm excitedly. "A European ship?" I asked quickly.

"Big ship," he replied. "We keep white men there from drowning."

"Are they still alive?"

"Yes, yes, they dwell at my nation."

This revelation put new thoughts into my head. I took Friday and hurried to the site where I had left my original canoe. I had hoped it might still be in good shape and we could use it to escape. But when we found the canoe we saw that it had rotted and the wood had split from the sun.

I explained to Friday that if we built a new canoe, we could travel far from here. So that very day we set out looking for a tree to fell. Friday knew what wood would be best and so he led me to a tree of Nicaragua wood. After cutting it down, I showed him how to carve out the cavity of the tree and to shape

I showed him how to carve out the cavity of the tree. . . .

the canoe. With Friday's help, the task that had once cost me three months of hard labor took only one. After this, it took us a fortnight to get it on rollers and so move it into the water.

I spent the next two months rigging and fitting the mast and sails. I even fixed a rudder to the stern to help me better steer the boat. It was during this work that I observed my twenty-seventh year of captivity of this place. I reflected on the good fortune that the previous year had brought. If Friday had not arrived on my island, I might well have forgotten how touching true friendship can be. A man never had a more faithful, loving, and sincere friend than Friday.

I thought that if our boat failed and I never left this place again, that I could be happy here with just Friday and myself. But this tranquil life was not to continue.

One day as I was gathering turtles and turtle eggs on the shore for the voyage away from the island, Friday raced up to me. "O sorrow! O bad!" he cried out again and again.

"What is the matter, Friday?" I said.

"Out yonder, there," he said, pointing out to sea. "One, two, three canoe! One, two, three!"

I looked to where he pointed and saw what he feared, canoes full of savages coming to the island.

"Friday," I said. "We must fight. Will you help me?"

"Me shoot," he said, his eyes wide with fear, "but there come many great number."

"Don't worry, those that we don't kill will be frightened by our guns."

We hurried back up the hill to retrieve our weapons. I took up a cutlass and four muskets, which I loaded with two lead slugs and five small bullets. I loaded my pistols with shot as well. I then handed to Friday one pistol and two muskets, which he slung over his shoulder.

We entered into the forest and made our way near to the shore.

"Friday," I whispered, "get closer if you can and tell me what they are doing."

He crept up noiselessly and returned to tell me that the savages sat around a fire and that they had a white man as a captive.

I assumed that it must have been one of the whites that Friday had told me came to his land. The thought that they might kill him filled me with dread. I had not a moment to lose. I snuck along the edge of the shore, hoping that the sound of the surf and the fire the savages made would mask the sound of my approach. I counted around the blaze a grouping of nineteen dark-skinned men.

"Friday," I said softly, "do exactly as you see me do."

So I set down one of the muskets upon the ground and Friday did likewise. I aimed the other musket at the savages.

"Fire!" I yelled as I emptied my gun with a loud blast. Friday leveled his weapon and did the same.

Instantly they leapt to their feet, except for the three we killed and five others who were wounded. But they did not know which way to run, or even where to look.

I took up the cutlass and a pistol, and Friday grasped his pistol.

"Are you ready, Friday?" I asked.

"Yes."

"Then fire again!"

With that I charged at the shocked wretches and so did Friday. We only dropped two more, but so many were wounded that they ran about yelling and screaming like wild creatures. I ran directly at the bound prisoner while the men who stood guard over him fell back in amazement. One jumped directly into the ocean while three more sprang to their canoes to escape.

While my man Friday fired at them, I released the binding that held the prisoner's feet and hands together. He was so faint and weak that he could

scarcely stand or speak, so I rubbed his wrists and moved his arms to get the blood flowing through them again. I asked him what country he was from.

"Espagniole," he replied.

"Señor," I said with as much Spanish as I could remember, "we will talk later. Now we must fight." He quickly regained his strength and with a sword that I gave him pounced upon his captors. With great fury, he cut two of them to pieces in an instant. Four others got into their canoes and began to paddle away.

I was very worried about the four escaping and returning with more men so I leapt into one of their canoes to follow them. To my shock, I found another poor creature lying on the canoe's floor, bound hand and foot.

I immediately cut the rushes with which he had been bound, but he was not strong enough to stand or speak. "Friday," I yelled out.

When Friday approached I asked him to speak to the freed man. But when Friday saw him, his eyes grew wide and he embraced the man. In fact, he kissed him, hugged him, laughed, jumped about, danced, sang, and then cried. I stared at my friend in astonishment.

"He is," Friday said between tears, "my father!"

It is not easy for me to explain the joy I felt in seeing Friday reunited with his father. I realized that it is something that I could never expect to do with my father. He was sickly when I left and since all the years that I have spent on this island, he surely must have died.

I lifted Friday's father very gently out of the canoe and fed him some bread and corn that I had with me. Friday raced home for a clay jug of fresh water.

At the end of the day, we had killed fifteen savages at the Battle of Crusoe's Island, as I named our skirmish, and doubled the population of my kingdom.

With that I charged at the shocked wretches. . . .

Chapter Twelve

My island now had four souls upon it, and I thought myself very rich to have so many people around me. I spoke at length with the Spaniard and found out that there were sixteen more of his countrymen who had been cast away and had learned to live in peace with the natives. He told me time and again how he wished to go back to them. After he returned to them, he said that he would send more back to rescue me.

When I felt he was strong enough, I agreed to his plan. We loaded up the canoe that I had made with Friday and put in it plenty of food for him to survive the voyage. Friday's father thought it made sense that he return with the Spaniard to the mainland. He believed he would be better able to keep them from landing in areas where they might be attacked by hostile savages. This made sense to me, although Friday was sad to see his father go. His father assured Friday that he would come back as soon as he could.

I gave them each a musket, and about eight charges of powder and ball in case they should be met by any murderers at sea.

I waited patiently for their return, knowing it might take over a week for the Spaniard to organize his men and find their way back to us. Therefore, I was surprised when Friday rushed up the hill one morning soon after they left, shouting at me.

"They are come, they are come," he said again and again.

I jumped up and got my clothes on. I was amazed when I looked out at the sea to see a large European ship about two and half leagues off shore. My heart was about to burst from my chest in excitement when I regained my senses.

"Friday," I shouted, "get inside the cave! We do not know if they are friends or enemies yet."

Both Friday and I stared at the ship anchored off our little island before I thought to fetch my perspective glass. We climbed to the top of our hill, careful not to be seen. When at last I took a look at them from my glass, I was relieved to find it was an English ship. I cannot express the joy I felt at seeing a vessel manned by my own countrymen.

I raced down the hill. As I did so, I noticed a longboat full of men leave the ship and begin toward the island.

"I am here!" I yelled. "I am here!" Though I knew they could not hear me, I could not contain my delight that I was being rescued. I half-ran, half-leapt down the hill to welcome my countrymen to my island. Saved! I thought. At last I'm saved.

The longboat ran ashore about a half mile from me and I was about to burst out of the forest when I saw the strangest of sights. I stopped short.

Eleven men got out of the boat, but three were bound and unarmed.

"Look," I whispered to Friday. "Those three men are being held against their will—I fear the others intend to murder them."

We both watched, from the privacy of the forest, as the armed men scattered in every direction on the shore, as if they wished to see the country they had just landed on. The three bound men were allowed to walk where they pleased, but as they were bound, they simply sunk down upon the ground, like men in despair.

The sea was at the high-water mark when these people landed on my island. For a while the eight unbound men scurried about on shore, running and drinking rum and generally clearly happy to be out of the confines of their ship. After they exhausted themselves running about, they sat down beneath the shade of a tree. Friday and I watched nervously, waiting to see what they would do next. As they rested, the hours slipped by and the tide began to go out, until at last, it hit the low-water mark, leaving the boat grounded and unable to be moved. I knew it would be no less than ten hours before the boat could be set out to sea again, and by that time it would be getting dark and I hoped to be able to get closer and possibly hear their plans.

Meanwhile, I prepared myself for battle. I saw several of the men had pistols and since I couldn't yet decide whether they were friendly or not, I thought it best to be prepared. I took two fowling pieces for myself, and gave Friday three muskets. At two o'clock in the afternoon they lay down to sleep in the shade. The three unarmed men, appearing too worried to get any sleep, sat underneath a tree apart from the rest.

I came as near as I could to them and called to them softly in Spanish.

"Where are you from?" I asked.

They were startled at the noise, and even more amazed when they saw me, dressed in goat skin, clutching my guns. I spoke to them again in English.

"Gentlemen, do not be surprised, for you have found a friend."

"You must be from heaven," said one of them, "because our fate is beyond the help of a man."

"All help is from heaven, sir," I whispered. "I am an Englishman, so tell me, what happened to you?"

"Kind sir," he replied, with tears running down his face, "I was the commander of that ship. My men have mutinied and have set me with these two loyal men on shore."

"I saw one of the brutes that brought you on shore raise a sword as though in threat to kill you earlier," I said, untying their hands.

"They meant to scare me even more," the captain said, happy to be free from the ropes that bound his wrists. "But they will not kill us. It is their plan to leave us here, which is just as good a death."

"It is not that bad!" I laughed.

"If the two leaders are killed or captured," said the commander, "I believe the other men will surrender and return to their duty."

"Then that is what we must do. Let us retreat out of their view in case they wake up." So the three men went with me into the security of the forest where we joined Friday. I handed them each a musket.

"Here is powder and ball also. The best way to attack is all at once."

The commander of the ship took the musket I offered him as well as a pistol which he stuck in his belt. I thought it best to stay behind with Friday until we were needed.

Now fully armed, the commander and his men crept back out of the forest and up to the mutineers. One of the seamen awoke and cried out to the rest, but it was too late. For the moment he called out, my men fired. The man died on the spot. One of his companions near to him was wounded severely in the chest, and another was wounded in the arm, and a third had his head grazed by a shot. He fell back onto the sand, holding his bleeding ear.

When at last I dashed from the woods with Friday on my heels, these men saw that they were outnumbered.

"Mercy!" they cried. "Have mercy on us."

"If I spare your lives, do you swear to be faithful to me?" asked the captain.

They readily nodded their heads that they would.

While this was happening, Friday and I secured the longboat on the shore, and hid away the oars and sail. I brought the captain and his men up to my home and gave them some food. While we ate, we discussed what the other mutineers on the ship would do when their comrades did not return from the island.

"Surely," said the captain, "they will try and signal the men on shore to return." No sooner had he said this than the sound of guns came from the ship. Twice more gunshots rang out before a longboat was lowered. I got out my perspective glass and saw ten men with firearms on board.

We marched down from the hill to meet these men, keeping out of sight so that we could surprise them.

When the men reached the shore, eight got out and started to shout out "Halloo!" and "Are ye here?" But there was no reply.

All but two left the boat and began to march inland. But they did not get far, seemingly fearful to leave the relative safety of the boat. After a half an hour, they looked around once more, then gathered beneath a tree.

"Friday," I said, "take the captain's mate, go over to the creek, and shout, 'Halloo!' to those men. When they come toward you, go father off and shout out again, always keeping out of sight. Draw them as far into the island as you can."

The eight sailors were just returning to their boat when Friday called out for the first time. The men raced after the shouts, disappearing into the woods.

After they were gone, I took the captain and the rest of his men to the boat on the shore. We had our pistols out and were ready to fire, but the two sailors in the boat were fast asleep, tired from the hot sun. We awoke them and took them as our captives back into the woods.

It was several hours before Friday and the captain's mate returned. Friday was grinning and appeared very happy with himself.

"From one wood to the other they chased us," he said. "We waited until all were tired and sat. Then shouted again. Again they would stand and chase us."

"Wonderful," I said to my friend. "Where are they now?"

"They coming right behind. They here in a minute."

And in a few moments the six men came out of the woods toward the boat. They called to their men, but received no answer. Then they stood around confused, looking at the empty boat stranded by the low tide. Again they called out to their two companions, and again were answered only by silence.

The hour was late and the island was growing dark as we sat and discussed how we could subdue these men. I was against attacking them in the dark because I didn't want to lose the life of a single man in our party. We knew they were well armed, so we decided to wait until we could separate them.

At long last, the leader of the mutiny came walking toward where we were hidden in the woods. The captain was so eager to get this man that he leapt from the hiding place. Friday was right behind him, and together they fired their pistols. The shots rang out over the silence of the island, and in the flash of gunpowder we all sprang out with guns blazing.

I was lucky enough to see the face of the main mutineer before he collapsed onto the beach and died. In the last instant of his life, in the flash of gunpowder he saw the face of the captain coming at him, triumphant at last. The look of surprise, no, horror, was something I will never forget.

I advanced with my army upon the other men, who could not see how many we were in the dark. I fired a shot over their heads and they quickly begged for mercy. The captain advanced to them as they laid down their pistols.

"You men thought you were leaving your captain on a deserted isle," he began. "But you and the leaders of your mutiny were wrong. The Governor of this island (he meant me) is an Englishman. I will plead your case before him, asking him if it is all right that you return to the ship and swear again to be loyal. If you do this, I will ask him that you not be hung like dogs."

The men shuffled and spoke among themselves. I had a grin on my face they could not see, because I had never before been called "Governor."

The mutinous men agreed. They all returned to the ship. As soon as the ship was secured, the captain ordered seven guns to be fired. This was the signal that would tell me that everything was fine and that they were successful. I climbed up to my house on the hill for the very last time.

CHAPTER THIRTEEN

I slept soundly that night. Early the next morning I was awoken by somebody climbing my hill, calling out "Governor, Governor." It was the captain, and my day of deliverance had finally arrived!

We walked together to the top of the hill and there we stood for a few moments. At last he pointed to the ship and said, "My dear friend and deliverer, there's your ship. She is all yours." We embraced and I thanked him for his kindness.

The ship, anchored not far from shore, was a mighty sight.

"Captain," I said, "you were surely sent from heaven to deliver me. I thank the eyes of the Infinite Power to have seen me in the most remote corner of the world. In His kindness, he sent you to me."

When I left the island later that day I carried on board things that were dear to me that would help me remember my time there always. Among those items were my goat-skin cap and umbrella that I made, and my parrot. Friday came along with me as well. I intended to sail to his land so that he could be reunited again with his father. That way we could also save the Spaniard and his companions.

And thus I departed the island on the nineteenth of December in the year 1686. I had been upon it twenty-eight years, two months, and nineteen days. In this vessel, after a long voyage, I arrived in England on the eleventh of June, 1687, after having been absent for thirty-five years.

. . . I thanked him for his kindness.